Bianca, Or, The Young Spanish Maiden

Bianca, Or, The Young Spanish Maiden

Toru Dutt

MINT EDITIONS

Bianca, Or, The Young Spanish Maiden was first published in 1878.

This edition published by Mint Editions 2021.

ISBN 9781513299983 | E-ISBN 9781513223421

Published by Mint Editions®

 MINT EDITIONS

minteditionbooks.com

Publishing Director: Jennifer Newens
Design & Production: Rachel Lopez Metzger
Project Manager: Micaela Clark
Typesetting: Westchester Publishing Services

"Féicité passé
Qui ne petit revenir,
Tourment de la pensée,
Que n'ai-je en te perdaut, perdu le souvenir!"

CONTENTS

I

It was a cold, drizzling day of February. The bare trees waved their withered branches to the biting wind, in a weird and mournful manner, as if they were wringing their hands in agonised despair.

A funeral procession was winding slowly up the path; two mourners followed the coffin; the church yard was in a lonely place; so there were no half-curious, half-sympathising people following. It was the daughter of Alonzo Garcia a foreign gentleman residing in England, his eldest daughter and his most loved; the youngest was by his side, Bianca. She did not weep; she was calm and quiet, and followed her father with a downcast race; no tear was there in her eye.

The Rector, Mr. Smith waited at the vestry he shook Mr. Garcia's hand but did not utter a word. He also took Bianca's hand in both of his, in a fatherly way; his grasp, his kindly look, brought the tears to her eyes, and she bent her head lower. Then they all followed the Bad procession. Through the drear wind and falling snow, clear, soft, mournful yet comforting was heard the voice of Mr. Smith. "I am the resurrection and the life, saith the Lord: he that believeth in me, though he were dead, yet shall he live: and whosoever liveth and believeth in me shall never die."

"I know that my Redeemer liveth, and that he shall stand at the latter day upon the earth. And though after my skin worms destroy this body, yet in my flesh shall I see God: whom I shall see for myself, and mine eyes shall behold, and not another."

"We brought nothing into this world, and it is certain we can carry nothing out. The Lord gave, and the Lord hath taken away; blessed be the name of the Lord."

"I said, I will take heed to my ways: that I offend not in my tongue."

"I will keep my mouth as it were with a bridle: while the ungodly is in my sight."

Mr. Smith stopped; father and daughter lifted their eyes; they had arrived at the place of rest.

Now the procession stopped; Miss Garcia stooped down to place a wreath of white roses on the coffin; two small buds fell from the garland to the ground; she took them up and kept them within her hand. 'Twas dead Inez' gift to her; thought she.

They lowered the coffin. The father stood, silent, his eyes half-closed, his lips trembling; was he praying? was he weeping? Bianca's tears fell silently, drop by drop; sometimes a deep-drawn sigh shook her slight frame; she kept down the sobs in that way. The first lump of earth was thrown over the pale blue colored coffin; it was soon invisible. The grave was filled. Everyone went away. Father and daughter stayed some minutes longer; at last Miss Garcia took her father's hand in her own. "Come away father, come home." He went with her docilely. She turned back her head once more; oh, she longed to go and lay herself down on the newly made grave, and die there.

They came home. The father went straight to the room whence the dear dead had been borne away, where she had passed her last days. His daughter did not follow. She knew she could do nothing to console him. God even cannot, sometimes. Let the mourner remain alone with the Divine Comforter: He will give him peace and strength to bear the sorrow. Bianca entered her own room. She sat by the window; a book lay open on the table; her eye fell upon it; Inez was very fond of it; it was Tennyson's *In Memoriam*. The first lines Bianca came upon were:

> *Come, let us go, your cheeks are pale,*
> *But half my life I leave behind*
> *Methinks my friend is richly shrined,*
> *But I shall pass; my work will fail.*
>
> *Yet in these ears till hearing dies,*
> *One set slow boll will seem to toll*
> *The passing of the sweetest soul*
> *That ever looked with human eyes.*
>
> *I hear it now, and o'er and o'er,*

How often had she heard Inez repeat these lines in her soft silvery voice,

> *I hear it now, and o'er and o'er,*
> *Eternal greetings to the dead;*
> *And "Ave, Ave, Ave", said,*
> *"Adieu, adieu" for evermore!*

She closed the book and looked out of the window. Where was Inez now? Beneath the cold earth:—She so delicate was now sleeping quietly in the wild churchyard with nothing between her and the inclement sky, but a thin oak-plank, and the newly turned sod. Bianca's heart "*se serra*" convulsively at the thought. Why should *she* so strong be housed from the weather in a warm, lighted room, while pale Inez lay cold and stiff in the lonely grave-yard? She looked with drear despair at the drizzling snow and rain. Her large eyes were dilated; she opened the window (it was a glass door) and stept out into the garden. She smiled, it was a strange, peculiar smile, "I am like you now Inez dear," murmured she, and sat down on the soaked ground, her head bent down. How long she remained there she did not know.

It was getting dark when a hand was placed on her shoulder; and a voice, Martha's voice said. "Miss Bianca whatever are you at?"

She opened her eyes but without stirring. "Miss Bianca, Miss Bianca," cried Martha beseechingly, "Puir thing, puir thing, she does not hear." And Martha shook her by the shoulders. "Are ye benumbed, are ye frozen?"

She rose now. "No Martha; there's nothing the matter with me."

"But why are ye out, all alone, in the snow? If ye go on in this way, ye'll soon fallow sweet Miss Inez."

"Would to God, I could;" exclaimed she below her breath, and her brown eyes looked dreamily and longingly at the drear scenery around. "And if ye were baith to leave your auld father, what's to become of him I should like to know?" Martha said.

She turned her face towards the old Scotch woman. "You are right, Martha. Poor papa," she murmured, and got up.

"Ye are wet through Miss Bianca, ye must change your clothes."

"I'll take a cup of tea first Martha, and papa must have something." She entered the dining room.

Reader let me describe her to you a little.

She was not beautiful; of the middle height; her slight figure was very graceful; her face was not quite oval; her forehead was low; her lips wore full, sensitive and mobile; her colour was dark; have you ever soon an Italian peasant girl? When she blushed or was excited, the color mounted warm and deep to her pale olive cheek; she was beautiful then; her dark brown eyes—"just like Keeper's" (the dog's) her father would say, smiling—were large and full; in fact this pair of eyes and her long, black curls were her only points of beauty.

Martha brought her a cup of tea, she took it; then made one large cup for her father and went upstairs. She hung up her dress; her father must not see her thus drenched—he would be anxious. Then she softly entered the room where the much-loved had died. Her father was on his knees beside the bed; she put the cup gently on the side-table, and came quietly and knelt beside him. Some time elapsed; she was weeping silently to herself; when a hand was placed heavily and slowly on her shoulder. She knew it was her father's. A thrill of unknown pleasure she felt at this touch. He had never caressed her; Inez had been his favourite.

He loved both his daughters, but Inez with her childlike grace, her utter dependence on him, her caressing ways, had been his best-loved; Bianca although younger, was so grave, so sedate, so womanly, so independent, that he looked on her as his counsellor; sometimes even he would ask her advice in some important matter; "she was his right hand" he would say, "as good as a son to him; beneath her girl's boddice beat a heart as bold as any man's; beneath her wavy curls was a head as sharp and intelligent as any mathematician's." Inez was the being to whom both were devoted; father and sister worshipped Inez. Sometimes Bianca felt a pang when she saw her father pass his hand on his eldest daughter's shoulder; or, but this was very rarely, for M. Garcia was not a demonstrative man, kiss her on the cheek.

"After all, he loves Inez best," Bianca would think awake in her bed; "and is not that right? Inez wants to be looked after; she is so loving; no wonder he loves her best. I should not be jealous; I am strong; I can take care of myself."

During Inez's illness no mother could have been a better nurse than young Bianca was. It was a wonder how she would keep awake three or four nights running; she never left the house even for a walk; sometimes she would go out to buy some grapes or pears—Inez was so fond of fruits. Much-loving, much-loved Inez!

M. Garcia rose at last. "Come Bianca, she is at peace now."

They both went out; she took him to the parlour; and gave him the cup of tea. He did not take further notice of her; he was looking at the stars.

After a pause, he said, half to himself. "But last Tuesday, she was with us, and now beyond the stars! How strange it all seems."

A silence. Presently she said quietly, "your tea is getting cold, father, drink it." He did so, and pushed the cup towards her; she filled it again. "It is refreshing" he said.

They remained silent for the space of about two hours engrossed in thought. Bianca coughed several times while both were so absorbed. "Have you got a cold Bianca?" said her father anxiously.

TORU DUTT

"A slight one, father."

"How did you catch it? you must take great care of yourself, now my child," and he put his hand out to her; she put her's in it, and came and sat quietly beside him on a low stool at his feet. Presently she said, "Father shall I read to you?"

"Yes, do. Take something warm before you go to bed tonight."

"Yes, father; what shall I read? The 14th chapter of John?" He nodded, and she opened the book. In her soft yet rich tones she read, "Let not your heart be troubled, neither let it be afraid. Ye believe in God, believe also in me. . ."

When she had finished the chapter, she closed the book slowly. They then knelt down and prayed. "Now Bianca, go to bed."

He rang the bell. "Martha get Miss Bianca something warm, she has got a bad cold."

"No wonder she has with—"

Bianca interrupted her; "come away Martha." Outside the dining room; "Martha," said she, "you must not tell father where I was this morning."

"Very well, Miss Bianca," she replied.

Martha brought her young mistress a cup of hot spiced wine. Bianca drank it, then she went upstairs. She went towards the door of her sister's room, she turned the lock slowly and entered. She half expected to see Inez there in her white robe lying quiet and pale in her coffin, with her arms across her breast, and her dark, soft hair framing her peaceful, beautiful face, and her lips half-open in a calm, gentle, and happy smile. She had seen her thus last night. Bianca knelt beside the bed and prayed. She came out half an hour afterwards; a step was mounting the stairs; she passed quickly and silently to her own room. She heard the steps stop before the door. Would he go in? No. He went to his own bedroom.

Next morning when Bianca awoke, she involuntarily turned her face towards the bed where Inez used to sleep before her illness. She turned her head away presently with a sigh; she got up and kneeling at the foot of the bed, wept, with her head buried in the counterpane. She did not pray. "Inez come back"—that was her cry, wrung from her heart. By and by the tears dropped slower.

She was thinking.

"How happy she is!" thought she, "in that garden full of flowers, as she said; how happy she is, with dear mother walking beside her. Is the garden very beautiful, Inez?"

And again the bitter cry went forth, "Inez take me with you! I feel so very wretched! She knelt there sometime; gradually a sense of numbness came over her; her eyes became dry. She got up, dressed, and sat down before the open window. "Father must not see that I have cried."

The cold morning air soon dissipated all the traces of tears and she went downstairs. "Is not father risen yet, Martha?" She asked surprised at finding the dining-room empty.

"No Miss."

She went upstairs and tapped at her father's door, "Shall I come in, father?"

"Yes."

She entered. "Why! Still in bed father! Are you ill?"

"Yes Bianca; feel my forehead and hands child."

She did so. They were burning hot. "You have got the fever father; I must send for the doctor."

Her father passed his hand over her head. "What would you do Bianca, if I were to leave you and die?" said he half jestingly.

"You are not going to die father, I won't let you," she said, smiling, but she turned her face away to hide the rising tears.

He sighed. "But to me it would be the best thing, I ask nothing but to be at rest."

"I must get you something warm father" rising, she said, "and write to the doctor."

She went out and shut the door after her. On the staircase she stopped a few minutes, then entered her own bedroom and sat down in a chair. The tears fell fast.

Will he indeed die? "God," she thought, "give me a sign that he will live. Oh God! Think this not presumptuous but give faith to thy servant and strengthen her."

She knelt down and opened the Bible. The words which struck her eye were: "Behold I will bring it health and cure, and I will cure them, and will reveal unto them the abundance of peace and truth." She read the passage again and again with a happy smile, while the tears were still bright her wet cheek; then she kissed the words and closed the book. "Lord, I thank Thee," said she, with her forehead leaning on the "Gospel of peace." She was strengthened. She came down, wrote to the doctor, and then brought M. Garcia his tea.

P resently there was a tap at the door, and Martha entered. "Please sir, there is Mr. Smith waiting downstairs, will he come in?"

"By all means. Bianca bring him here. I should like to see him."

Bianca went down. Mr. Smith was waiting in the hail. The front door was open, and gusts of fresh wind were sweeping in. Mr. Smith took Bianca's two hands in his own.

"And how is papa?"

"He is very ill; he wants to see you Mr. Smith."

"Ill! I am sorry to hear that. What is the matter with him?"

"Fever." And the girl's eyes filled.

"Poor child! Poor child!" said the Rector patting her on the head; "God will give you strength to bear all this. His grace is sufficient for us."

He followed her upstairs. The Rector went to the bedside of the patient. They did not talk much, but the silent and sincore sympathy apparent in Mr. Smith's mild face was more welcome than a host of words from any of Job's comforters.

Bianca sat by the window. The doctor presently came. He prescribed; then went away; he was a busy man.

A week past, a week of intense bodily and mental suffering; on the seventh day M. Garcia opened his eyes, and recognised his daughter. He almost started at first. Her pale profile, as she sat quietly by the window recalled his lost Inez vividly to his mind.

"Come here, Bianca."

She went and put her hand in his, he grasped it warmly and tears came into the eyes of both. God had been merciful to Bianca.

II

More than twelve months had passed. It was a bright June day. A young man and woman were sauntering thoughtfully in the fields. It was Bianca and Mr. Walter Ingram.

"Look Mr. Ingram isn't the sun beautiful? The west seems lightened by a bonfire."

He turned half round: "Yes; it is very beautiful;" he said.

He was a rather handsome young man of about twenty four, with a frank countenance, fair hair, and pale blue eyes; his lips were full, but they lacked firmness; in stature he was of the middle height. There was pause. Bianca was looking dreamily at the far west when the voice of her companion interrupted her reverie.

"Bianca" he said. "I want to tell you something important; shall we go first to a quieter spot?"

"This is quiet enough. Say on." And she turned towards him.

He had bent his head and with his cane was writing thoughtfully on the ground. He was so long speaking, that she got impatient.

"Well?" She said.

"Bianca," he said and his voice was very low, and his utterance quick, "will you be my wife? I should be so happy with you."

She shook her head, a faint peculiar and rather sad smile parted her lips. "You loved *her* Walter; Inez was to have been your wife; she has left us all; the angels loved her too; poor Walter!" For he had turned his face away. "Your obligations to papa, I should say your gratitude rather, makes you think that you must marry one of his daughters. With Inez it was different, and all right. *She* loved you and you loved her."

"But I think I love you too Bianca."

"Well, I don't love you, I like you, that is all. Yes, I like you very much, as a friend and a brother. If she had lived, poor Walter!" And she placed her hand on his shoulder.

He sat down and buried his face in his hands. She sat down too beside him; she saw the tears trickling through his fingers.

"Poor fellow! Poor boy!" she murmured; and she took one of his hands in hers. "You loved her as much as that! I did not know it Walter, I thought she loved more than she was loved." Bye and bye he quieted down. "I did not know how much I loved till I lost her!" "And you wanted to marry me Walter, what if I had said yes." And she smiled one little smile to herself. "I should not have been sorry. I should have taken you at your word. Even now you are the woman I should select as a wife if I had to choose from the whole world. You know me and my ways, you can help me in my struggle through life."

"Can I? I shall help you as a sister, brother. Walter, you must come to me in your difficulties."

"Yes indeed, I shall sister Bianca."

"Now get up Walter, I must be going home."

They walked together a few yards.

"There is Maggie coming" said Bianca, shading her eyes; then, as if a new sudden thought had struck her. "Walter that is the girl you ought to marry. She is just the wife for you."

"Isn't that Miss Moore?"

"Yes! why! you know her already!"

"Yes I met her once or twice. I know her brother a little."

Miss Moore came running to her friend. "Now Bianca," said she, kissing her in her warm girlish way, I have a bone to pick with you. You haven't come to see us for a long time." Then seeing Mr. Ingram, she gave him her hand, then turning again to her friend. "When will you come? You know Colin is away in London; and the house is so dull without him. Mamma keeps me at lessons. Will you come tomorrow Bianca. Say, yes."

"Yes Maggie."

"There's my own darling old Bianca. Good bye. Come early." And with a nod to Mr. Ingram she disappeared.

At the door Ingrain shook hands with Bianca. "You won't come in?"

"No, not today."

Then after a slight pause and reddening.

"Bianca, I behaved like a fool today, in asking you such a question. You forgive me, don't you?"

She nodded merrily; "I am glad you see it."

"It seems natural to you to be sister Bianca to every body. So goodbye sister Bianca."

"Goodbye Walter."

In the evening as she was sitting out in the garden with her father, she told him all. "Father, Ingram was wanting to marry me today."

He turned to her; "Indeed," said he, and the remembrance of Inez came to him.

"Yes father, and I refused him."

"You did well, child; he is a worthy boy, very good and frank; but I would not like you to marry him; he was well matched with Inez I should have given her to him gladly; but I look for a different man for you."

She smiled, pleased, at these words. "But I will never marry father. Life is full of care, and the lonelier you are, the easier is it to live and die."

"True, very true, in one sense." And her father sighed. After a pause he said. "And so the lad wanted to marry you! He did not love my Inez then?"

"In his own way, he did; he is very good, but he is not very steady. He is impressionable."

After another pause he murmured half to himself,

Ah! dear, but come thou back to me
Whatever change the years have wrought
I find not yet one single thought,
That cries against my wish for thee!

She went quietly and sat down beside him, with her sewing in her hand. He passed his hand over her hair. "It is better so," he said, "after all she is safer in the Master's fold than here."

After some cursory talk, Bianca as her custom was, brought a French book; her father read aloud from it and she sowed; then in her turn she read aloud and he listened. It was About's "Germaine." M. Garcia had been asked by the editor of a magazine to write an article on French light literature of the present day. A refugee, and in exile for a long time, he eked out his scanty income by writing occasionally for the press. A perfect knowledge of the literature of many countries qualified him well for such work.

"About is always 'spirituel,' isn't he father? Though his standard of morality isn't very high;" remarked Bianca "He is very epigrammatic, and the dullest subject he can make interesting as a novel. The 'Grece Contemporaine' is an instance."

"I don't wonder the Empress used to have him at her soirées to make him tell a tale impromptu. I should like to hear him."

As the night came on, they closed the book and remained silent. Bianca was looking at the moon. What were the thoughts passing through her head? It would be hard to tell. Her face was very thoughtful, yet there was a quiet brightness in it, and her eyes had a dreamy far-off look. She rose up suddenly, and a rather sad smile parted her lips.

"We must be going father, it is late."

They both went in; as she was going to bed she said; "Father, Maggie ask me to go and see her tomorrow; I may go?"

"Yes, by all moans. But stop—the old lady may think you want to hook her son as a husband."

She laughed, and her father smiled too. "He isn't here now, he is in London, father."

"Well, then you can go. When are you going?"

"Oh tomorrow; any time will do. Shall you want me tomorrow?"

"The article I am going to write should be looked at. I should like to have your opinion Bianca. I have to send it tomorrow."

"Oh I will look over it, and, then I shall go."

She said goodnight and went to her own room. She undressed and then sat down by the window, bye and bye she began repeating fragments of poetry.

> *"She was thinking of a hunter,*
> *From another tribe and country,*
> *Young and tall and very handsome,*
> *Who one morning, in the Spring-time,*
> *Came to buy her father's arrows,*
> *Sat and rested in the wigwam,*
> *Lingered long about the doorway,*
> *Looking back as he departed.*
> *She had heard her father praise him,*
> *Praise his courage and his wisdom;*
> *Would he come again for arrows*
> *To the falls of Minnehaha*
> *Minnehaha, laughing water?*
> *On the mat her hands lay idle*
> *And her eyes were very dreamy."*

Bianca's were. Presently with a smile; "I am getting sentimental; I mustn't say that 'young and tall and very handsome,' and think of him. Pooh! It can never be. Why do I think of him? It does me no good; on the contrary it does me harm. He is a lord of Burleigh. Now-a-days lords do not come to woo village maidens; and besides I am no village maiden; neither am I pretty. So be off,—all dreams never to be fulfilled,"—and half jestingly yet with rather a sad smile she went to bed. After a time she got up. "I have not prayed. How wicked I am getting." And kneeling down beside the bed, she prayed earnestly for forgiveness and peace; and then she went back to sleep.

III

Lady Moore received Bianca courteously, indeed the cold manner with which she used latterly to welcome the girl, was almost absent that day. Maggie came running out, all smile and welcome. Little Willie, he was my Lady's youngest, a posthummous child, and only four years old, came running also to Miss Garcia; she took him in her arms, and carried him to the drawing room. My Lady was very affable.

"I am glad to see you again, Miss Garcia, it is a long time since you called here last. You mustn't forget old friends. Willie is so fowl of you, he has been asking for you twenty times a day."

"Were you Will?" And the girl smiled brightly at the child.

Willie sat quiet; he was rather an absent-minded fellow: suddenly,— "Mista Ingwani cam he'e Cissey, this morning."

"Do you know him Will?"

Smiling, "yes; mamma and I saw him yeste'day. And you we'e the'e; you did not ohee me; we we's behind the t'ee."

My Lady rose up quickly; "Come Willie, you must want your dinner, it's past four o'clock. You just be hungry."

"No ma, I shall sit he'e."

"Now get down Master Willie," said Maggie; "I must show Bianca my flower beds."

"Then I'll go with you."

And Willie jumped off Bianca's lap.

My Lady was very gracious "Miss Garcia don't carry Willie, he is too heavy."

And Willie who was just stretching out his little stout arms, turned away in sullen wrath against—his mother. No; against Bianca! Bianca's allurements, all her loving phrases were lost upon him;

"You a'e weak; you cannot carry me; go away."

"You are strong Willie, aren't you?"

"Yes."

"Well give me a slap on my palm."

"It will hu't."

"I don't beleve it. Try."

The boy gave a slap with all his little might; Bianca winced with well-feigned pain; "Oh you hurt me." And she wrung her hand.

"Did not I tell you so!" Said Willie triumphntly. "Well, I shall want a strong arm to lean upon, will you lend me your's." Willie very proudly took in his little hand that of Miss Garcia; and thus peace being restored, they all repaired to the garden.

They had been walking about for some time; Miss Garcia had been running about in a side alloy with little Willie. Soon Maggie appeared looking for her.

"How flushed you are Bianca! Come and sit on the bench with mamma."

Bianca went with Willie in her arms. Lady Moore was seated on a rustic bench, with a small table before her, on which was placed a sumptuous little dinner for Master Willie.

"Now then come and eat your dinner Willie." Said his mother.

"Who'll cut me my meat and my bwead ma?" With a sly 'will-you' glance a Bianca.

"I will," said Miss Garcia. Willie was charmed.

"Now Will what will you take next?" as the soup and fish were dispatched with marvellous alacrity.

"You call me Will; I like that Bianca, Colin calls me Will."

When dinner was finished, Willie nestled in Bianca's lap, with a sigh. It was getting dark; Willie was bashful; that sigh meant a desire for a kiss from now that nobody was looking; Bianca kissed the smooth round cheek, that was pressed close against her's.

"I wish Colin was he'e;" said the boy.

"Your wish is fulfilled then, Willie, for there is Colin coming; it can't be but him," said Maggie Lady Moore turned her eagle eye towards the gate.

"It *is* Colin. We did not expect him today."

A tall form was striding quickly towards the group; Maggie ran forward; "O Colin this is kind! What a good brother you are!" And she hung caressingly on his arm; he kissed her on the forehead with a grave smile; then he went to his mother who kissed him in her freezing manner; Lady Moore loved her son passionately, but she was very undemonstrative.

"This is quite unexpected Colin; I thought you were not coming till Wednesday."

"I am not unwelcome, mother mine, am I?" asked he with his quiet smile.

"You know you are not, my boy."

"The fact is, I finished my business in London sooner than I expected, so I came home."

He turned towards Miss Garcia; she gave him her hand with a quiet, "How do you do?"

Little Willie who was reclining on her lap, with his curly head heavy with sleep near her shoulder, murmured half asleep; "Kiss me Co'in."

"Come to me then Will," and Lord Moore stretched his hands towards him.

"No; I am s'eepy; kiss me now, bofo'e I s'eep."

Lord Moore bent over the little face; his drooping brown hair almost touched Bianca's forehead as he kissed the child. There was a keen brightness in his hazel eyes, an unusual glow on his white forehead as he turned towards his mother. Her face was rigid and haughty as she made room for him beside her. She was the first to speak, and her voice was clear and cold, in spite of the polite manner.

"Miss Garcia you must feel cold with only that thin muslin dress on."

"No, my Lady, the evening is warm."

"And she looks so nice in white mamma," said Maggie smiling.

"There you are wrong Margaret; white suits fair complexions, and Miss Garcia is a dark beauty, dark as a gipsy I declare."

"Your father is Spanish, isn't he Bianca?"

"*Sangur azul*, Maggie," said Bianca, laughing.

"Has he really Moorish blood in his veins?"

"Yes, so it is believed."

"But if you are Spanish how do you know English so well, Bianca?" Asked Maggie.

"My paternal grandfather married an English lady, and my mother was an Englishwoman." Her voice lowered a little. "Your sister resembled your mother, I suppose; I only saw her once, she was very fair and beautiful."

Bianca did not reply.

Why should others speak of Inez, *her* and her father's Inez. It was a strange feeling, but she felt as if no one had a right to speak of Inez except her father and her sister. She presently said "I must go home." Then added; "Will has fallen fast asleep." And she rose taking Willie gently in her arms.

"Give him to me, he is too heavy for you." Said Lord Moore.

"No, thank you. It might awake him." Answered Bianca.

She entered the drawing room, unclasped the little arms from her neck, and as she did so sang or rather murmured unconsciously to herself (Bianca was passionately fond of poetry) some fragments of a song of which only these words were audible.

> By all the fond kisses
> I have given, By the plump little arms cleaving twine,
> By the bright eye whose language was heaven
> By the rose on the cheek pressed to mine.

Then she kissed the rounded cheek of her favorite and laid him gently on a couch and covered him carefully with a shawl. This done, she went out into the lawn, said good night to my lady and turned to Maggie, who kissed her warmly; "Good night, Bianca, will you come tomorrow?"

Bianca shook her head with a smile; "I cannot leave father alone every evening."

"Then day after tomorrow?"

"I won't promise, I dare say I shall not be able to come." She turned then to Lord Moore.

"I am going with you." He said.

"There is no need; there is moonlight to night."

"And it is not so far off, Colin."

"It is one good mile and more mother, and the village lads are rough and unmannerly." Bianca smiled; "Do you think I am not able to take care of myself, Lord Moore."

She had put on a long cloak over her dress; from a pocket in the lining she took out a small miniature pistol! "Look here!"

"What do you carry fire arms!" Cried Maggie aghast.

"The lads hereabouts are rough as my lord says; so father ordered this for me some months ago. He told me to have it always about me." And she put back the pistol in its hiding place.

"Well, I must have my own way," said Lord Moore smiling, "the night is very fine, and a little walk would be very pleasant."

So the two went forth. They were silent for some time; presently Lord Moore broke the silence.

"You are very fond of children, Miss Garcia."

"Not of all; indeed, not of any, except Will. Children do not seem to like me very much; I have lived so lonely with only my father for a companion, that I do not know how to make children love me. Little

Will seemed naturally to come to me; he loved me with his full pure little heart from the first day I saw him, and I love him too."

"You are a great reader of poetry, aren't you Miss Garcia? Maggie was telling me that you knew every poem that was ever penned even by the obscurest writer."

"Then Maggie was telling about things that she does not know for I am not so learned as that. Papa is somewhat of a poet; he wrote a volume of poems in Spanish some years ago; he contributes a piece or an article now and then to the Magazines?"

"What was the piece you were repeating while laying Will to sleep?"

"Were you in the room?" Said she surprised:

"No, I was sauntering at the door, did not you see me?"

"No, my lord." And she shook her head.

Since she was alone with him. Her manner had involuntarily changed towards him; she was subdued; she felt that this man walking by her side, had a power over her heart which perhaps he himself did not know. She loved him with all the fire and glow of her warm southern blood. Did he love her? She never asked the question to herself, she never thought of it. Sometimes a word from him would make her believe so, and then the red blood would send a dark flush on her olive cheek, a bright flash would come into her brown eyes, but she never let herself be deceived; a minute, a second, the cheek would glow and then become pale as usual.

"Would you mind repeating the piece to me?" Said Lord Moore.

"I do not remember it all. Papa has all the poems of the author of it, a Mr. Lloyd in his library. What I can remember, I shall repeat."

And in a rather hesitating and rapid voice she began, but as she went on, her tones became natural; she said the five or six verses she remembered, then added, "It makes one think of father;"

> *"And who—can I finish the story?*
> *Has seen them all shrink from his grasp,*
> *Departed the crown of his glory—*
> *No wife and no children to clasp!"*

She said this in a low tremulous voice not usual with her. Lord Moore did not reply; he continued to smoke his cigar in a thoughtful way. She was become very dear to his heart; this wild Spanish girl! Bianca went on; it seemed nothing strange to be speaking out her innermost thoughts to this man. She knew he understood them.

"We were six altogether, and now father has none but me, worthless me!" She said sorrowfully, almost passionately.

They sauntered on.

Presently, Lord Moore said, "How bright the moon's crescent is!"

"Some French poet compared it to a sickle dropped by angel mowers by chance,—a happy simile isn't it my lord?"

"Yes." Said he smiling. Her way of saying this "my lord" was very pretty. She had answered, when once questioned by him, that she merely translated "Signor" into English. He liked to hear her call him "my lord." It did not seem odd to him. "Look there is some one walking,—coming this way!" She said presently. The figure passed them swiftly, taking off its hat to Lord Moore.

"Who is it, my lord?"

"Mr. Owen, a cousin of ours. But hero we are at your home. Good night donna mia," with a smile, as he took her hand; "Goodnight, my lord." And he pressed the brown little hand in his broad white palm in a closer press perhaps, than the occasion warranted. As lie sauntered away buried in deep reverie he whistled to himself the air

"Oh saw ye not Bianca
She is gone into the West
To dazzle when the sun is down
And rob the world of rest."

He threw away his cigar. "She has robbed *me* of rest," thought he; then he smiled; "she *shall* be Lady Moore in spite of my mother."

When he came home, he entered his study and threw himself in an easy chair beside the open window.

"She *is* a little wild; so much the better; she is as nature made her. I like her *petits airs mutins*; her father has let her have her own ways in almost everything. I wonder if he'll part with her;" a cloud crossed his handsome brow; "it'll be a hard tug for *her* too; she is passionately fond of her father. I wonder if she'll consent to be my wife. I cannot live on without her. How confiding she is! And proud too. She can pay my lady in her own coin!"

And he smiled; "only the pride of Bianca is natural and innate; but my lady's—" He was interrupted by a tap at the door; "come in," he answered.

He was surprised to see his mother enter. He drew a chair for her near the window.

"Well, mother."

My lady coughed; looked at her son for full one minute; he was not at all subdued by this Gorgon gaze, as my lady thought he would be; his face became graver; the smile passed away from his lips; that was all. He expected what was coming.

"Colin, you are now twenty-five years old, you ought to think of settling down, my son."

"I quite agree with you, my mother; I am getting old; I shall soon want a wife to take care of me; but I think you can take care of your Colin in his dotage, can't you mother?" And he smiled pleasantly.

"Colin you are jesting; I am speaking in earnest. I *do* want you to marry and settle down."

"Whom shall I marry, mother?"

Lady Moore glanced quickly up at her son's face. He was looking out on the scene beyond, all shimmering in moonlight. His brow was contracted, his eye thoughtful. She read nothing in his face.

"There is Miss De Wilton." She said.

"Too old, mother, she must be twenty-five herself or more."

"She is rich; she will bring you fifty thousand pounds as dowry."

"I do not want money. She should marry a poor man, the curate."

"She is very beautiful."

"Tastes differ."

"She has beautiful auburn hair."

"Red, you mean, I like black better."

My lady's eyes shot an angry flash at her son, which was lost on him, for he was not looking at her. "And you like a sooty complexion, a snub nose, a low forehead, and a girl without a penny. But she cannot marry you; she is too far gone with—"

"Mother!" He turned upon her fiercely. There was no display of passion, but the tone of his voice, his vein-swollen forehead, the dark light in his hazel eyes silenced my lady.

She had never seen a man angry before. Her late husband was the mildest man in the world. Colin had been always to her at least "a careless but a good boy." She was subdued by his strange manner; she saw in him no more "the thoughtless lad" but a man, with the strong passions of a man. She felt she had gone too far.

He was the first to speak; he uttered his words slowly; "You must never speak against her before me, mother?"

"Why Colin?"

She had gained courage from his quiet manner; she did not know of the storm in his heart.

"Because I love her, mother; because I mean to marry her, mother; yes," he added, solemnly, "so help me God, she shall be my wife."

"Marry *her*! Marry a Spanish gipsy; an adventurer's daughter; she might have been a zingara for aught we know!"

He rose and to went the door. He was going out.

"Colin!" She called.

"Well?"

"I went say anything more against her, but listen to what I saw yesterday."

He leaned with his back against the door, expectant.

"She was speaking with Mr. Ingram, yesterday. He was saying something which moved him so much that he sat down on the ground, weeping, and she took his hands in hers and stroked and won't in a way—" my lady stopped, casting a sidelong glance at her son.

"Ingram was engaged to her sister," he replied calmly, "no wonder they were speaking of the dead."

My lady smiled. Such a venomous and wicked little smile it was! "So, she has been making you her confidant, the sly gipsy."

"Ingram told me about the affair, not she." He returned quietly.

There was a painful silence of some minutes.

"You have nothing more to say, mother?"

"No, Colin."

"Then good night, mother."

He took a candle and went out of the room. Lady Moore set her teeth and walked about the room in an agitated manner.

"The girl is nice in her way; but a Spanish gipsy! For I dare say she is nothing more, to marry my Colin! She isn't handsome, not at all. How can Colin love her. He must not marry her, no never. Perhaps the fit will pass off; but Colin is so steady, never was 'in love,' in his whole life. My course at least is clear. I must prevent such a marriage if possible." And my lady with a resolute expression in her face, went out of the room.

She tapped at her son's bedroom door, and on his calling out "come in," she entered. He was standing beside the window. He did not turn round at her step.

"Colin" said she, impetuously, "you must *not* marry that girl!"

"I am too far gone, mother," quoting half-unconsciously the words Lady Moore had herself applied not half an hour ago to Bianca.

"I suppose she has extracted a promise from you?"

He did not reply.

"You can break off with her, if you have imprudently committed yourself."

"Mother," he said turning round, "you weary me; I love her. Is not that enough? You always loved me; try to love her a little for my sake. You desire my happiness. I cannot be happy without her."

My lady did not reply, but with a cold good night quitted the room.

IV

More than a week after, Bianca was sitting in the garden, under a large laburnum; she was reading intently from a book on her knee; approaching footsteps made her look up; and a happy smile parted her lips as she greeted Lord Moore. Little Willie accompanied him. and ran up to Bianca, but suddenly stopped all crimson with pleasure and bashfulness; Bianca smoothed her lap in a most tempting manner; the boy laughed, "I went go," and darted back to his brother.

"Is your father in?" Asked Lord Moore.

"Yes, you will find him in his study."

"Now stay here Will; I shall soon be back." And he entered the house.

"Come to me, Will." Said Bianca.

"Neve'," said Willie, laughing and catching hold of the servant's (for *he* had his valet) hand.

"Go to Miss Garcia;" said John. Bianca knew the child thoroughly. She did not call him again, but pretended to be deeply buried in her book. The boy glanced slyly at her; she continued reading; he advanced a few steps, then ran back to John. She did not even raise her eyes; he came slowly and very quietly within her reach, and stood with his back turned towards her; she suddenly put her arms round him, and then he dropped, pat! into her lap; laughing and struggling. These little manuvres had happened over and over again to Will's never-ending delight.

"Now do be a little quiet, Will."

"I want those f'owe's, Bianca."

She rose and held him up in her arms; he plucked the golden bunches of laburnums with his sturdy little fingers; then laughing, he thrust them in her hair; she laughed, and gaining new ardour he plucked more and more of the "dropping gold" and thrust them within her raven looks; his two little hands were vigorously at work; when lo! the comb dropped off and the jot-black wavy looks foil all loose on her shoulders and down to her girdle.

"Oh how much hai'," said Willie in ecstasy.

"O Will, whatever have you done!"

"Neve'mind, dear, papa went be ang'y." She kissed him laughing, and was putting him down, when her father and Lord Moore emerged from the drawing-room.

"Why Bianca," cried Mr. Garcia, "how wild you look! All your hair is loose and all decked with flowers too, I declare!"

Lord Moore had bout down and was looking over the book which Bianca had been reading. "Will, did it father, unintentionally." Said she penitently.

"Go and bind it up then."

She was going away meekly. There was a harshness in Mr. Garcia's tone which hurt her, and almost brought tears of wounded pride to her eyes; she knew what was passing in her father's mind; she know that he thought that she was playing a little of the *coquette* before Lord Moore. Moore's voice arrested her.

"Stop one moment, Miss Garcia, I should like to ask you something about this book." She looked at her father. He nodded assent, and with a "Goodday." to Lord Moore re-entered the house.

"Come here, Miss Garcia." Said Lord Moore. She went to him and sat down by his side as he indicated. John came up.

"My lud; it's near four and Master William's dinner hour."

"Take him home then; I shall be at home in an hour." He kissed little Will, who kissed Bianca furtively and then disappeared in John's muscular arixs.

"It is a long time since you called, Miss Garcia."

"I could not go. What did you want to ask me about?"

"Oh, ay, the book; 'Lee Chatiments' by Hugo; is the poetry good?"

"Some parts are exceedingly good."

"Show them to me, if you please. You are not in a hurry to go, are you?"

Bianca had a slight qualm of conscience; would her father like to see her thus talking all alone for any length of time with Lord Moore; she knew that Mr. Garcia trusted her and had not the slightest fear to leave her alone in the wildest company, (she was brave) but he was afraid of people thinking him a husband-hunting father; he was mightily afraid of this;—but Lord Moore's manner was so kindly and so friendly!

"I shall read one or two passages, horn and there," she said, and taking the book, and turning over the leaves she began to read. At first, her voice was a little unsteady, but it grew firm and clear as she went on,

> *Devant les trahisons et les têtes coitrbéés,*
> *Jo eroiserai los bras, indigné, mais serein*
> *Sombre fidélité pour les choses tombées,*
> *Sois ma force ot ma, joie et mon pilior d'airain!*

Oui, tant qu'il sora là, qu'ou cède on qn'on persiste,
O France! France aimée ot qu'on pleure tonjours
Je ne roverrai pas ta terre douco et triste,
Tombeau do mes aïeux ot nid do mes amours!

Je ne reverrai ta rive qui nous tente,
France! hors le devoir, hélas! j'oublirai tout.
Parmi los éprouvés je plantoral ma tente:
Je resterai proscrit, voulant rester debout.

J'accepte l'âpre exil, n'eût-il ni fin ni terme;
Sans cherchor à savoir et sans considérer
Si quolqu'un a plié qu'on aurait cru pills ferme,
Et si plusieurs s'en vont qui devraieut demeurer.

Si l'on n'est plus quo mule, oh bien, j'en suis! Si mêmé
Ils no sout plus quo cent, je brave encore Sylla;
S'il en demeure dix, jo serai le dixième;
Et s'il n'en resto qu'un, je serai celui-là!

"How clear and ringing your voice is!" Lord Moore had bent over the book unperceived by Bianca.

She drew back shyly, and smiled. "I have got it from father, he is a capital reader."

There was a pause.

He rose and looked at his watch. "I must go now," said he. "Why do not you come and see us, sometimes; I shall be so happy to see you oftener at Moore-Rouse?"

She looked up at him and smiled gratefully. "But your mother does not like me, not much that is," she said assuming a careless air.

"Yes she does. . . and I do." He said the last words very low, and she did not hear them. She gave him her hand.

"Goodbye," said she; he had bent down to shake hands with her as she sat on the grass; he took her hand in his and looked into her face; a strange light, a deep passion was in his hazel eyes; impetuously, as if urged by an irresistible destiny, he stooped down and kissed her on the month. The instant after, he was gone. Bianca looked after him.

A strange feeling of unutterable bliss mingled with pain came upon her; "Oh, if he would kiss me again!"

She felt as if she had drunk of the heavenly hydromel of the poets, she wanted to take a deeper draught of the drink of the gods. She had never been kissed by a man. Mr. Garcia had not kissed her once since she was four years old. How strange, how soul-thrilling that touch of his ups was. It sent all the dark blood rushing to her olive cheeks and forehead. She buried her face in her hands and wept. Was it for joy or for sorrow? She felt as if she had committed a great sin. It seemed all so strange to her!

"How shall I tell father, for I *must* tell him! Oh how shall I tell him! How *could* he do it,—how could he? He shouldn't have done it." She murmured, the tears in her eyes; but she smiled through them, presently.

"How warm and strange his lips were, pressed close, close to mine." She sighed and rose; "I must tell father."

Mr. Garcia was in his study when Bianca entered his room. He looked up, smiling; "Well, what do you want, child—Why, you have been crying—what for?"

She came and kneeling beside him, with bent head, took his hand. "Father," said she, "Lord Moore kissed me today."

"The devil he did!" He exclaimed, taking away his hand from hers.

"What more?"

"Nothing more, father."

"Where was it?"

"On my lips, father."

"No—no—I mean where did all this happen?"

"In the garden, father, just now."

His angry manner frightened her; she was sobbing.

"What's the use of crying," said he angrily. "Shame on you! I thought you had more spirit than suffer a man to insult you!"

She turned round; her tears were checked; there was a deep fire in her eyes.

"Father, he did not insult me! Have you forgotten my cousin Maria?"

"No. You behaved bravely then, Bianca." And his voice softened a little; "as bravely, as gallantly as any man. You saved her honor."

"Father, I did not think it was wrong; he loves me so, and I—"

"Love him, too."

She tried to laugh, but it ended in a sob, and she turned her face away. There was a knock at the door.

"Who is it?" Asked Garcia angrily.

"It's I Martha; there's a letter from the Hall, sir."

He rose and went to the door.

"The servants mustn't see you thus distressed; what will they think?" muttered he to his daughter. He opened the door, took in the letter and barred the door. "I suppose it is an offer of marriage" said he, tearing open the envelope. He read it, then throw it to Bianca. "Read that; what *am* I to do! The world is full of troubles! The sooner one is out of it, the better."

Bianca wiped her eyes and took the letter. A feeling of a momentary pleasure sent the blood tingling to her cheeks; *he* had written it; her hand trembled a little as she held it; it was short.

> Dear Sir,
>
> Perhaps you have already perceived my feelings towards your daughter. I love her deeply, indeed, more than I can say. I ask her hand in marriage. Do not think I am hasty; I have known her long, and know her to be a far better woman than I deserve; but my love shall cover all my short-comings.
>
> I shall call for an answer during the evening. I pray God earnestly that He may direct you in forming your decision on my suit.
>
> Your's very faithfully,
> Henry Montague Moore

"Well!" said Garcia.

She did not reply.

"What am I to do?" he continued; "what will Lord Moore's mother think of me, if I allow my daughter to marry her son?"

She was looking away from him; "Never mind, what she thinks father; he loves me, that is all there is needed."

"But he is immensely rich, we have just enough to live upon."

"Oh father, let not money stand between me and my happiness!" She cried involuntarily.

"*Your happiness*! Aren't you happy? Ah! They have all left me, but *they* went to God, their heavenly Shepherd called them and they obeyed His voice, but *you* leave me for a man; they loved their Heavenly Father, more than their earthly one, and you love another man better than me!" And a deep sigh escaped him.

The tears started to her eyes,—"No, not better, father,"—she said slowly;—"but oh God! I shall be *now* so miserable without *him*."

"So should I be if you left me to marry this Lord Moore."

She buried her face in her hands for a few minutes then raising her face (it was very pale) towards Mr. Garcia. "Father," she said trying to speak calmly, "I will not marry him; I wish your peace and happiness above all things." She stopped.

"But just now you said you would be miserable without him you are very changeable."

"I shall not be *very* miserable as long as I have you father."

And kissing his hand meekly yet quickly, she went to the door and went out. Somebody was entering the passage at that moment; somebody very tall, who came up to her hastily and took both her hands in his and stooped down to read her face; she started back with a cry of pain; "Oh don't do it again, don't!" she said piteously; "I have sinned and father is so angry."

"Is it even thus!" He exclaimed; he opened the door of the study and entered; she went slowly upstairs into her own room, there to be alone with her despair and with her God.

Garcia looked up at the entrace of Lord Moore; he had been sitting quite thoughtful after his daughter had gone out.

Would the girl be really unhappy if he did not permit her to marry Lord Moore? She had been a very good child to him; never gave him a moment's trouble or anxiety all these eighteen years. She used to make light of marriage and love before; why the other day even, she was laughing about Ingram's offer to her. I thought I understood her thoroughly, but I find I am wrong; women are hard enigmas; if it had been a boy, I would have known how to manage and behave; but with a girl—Poor child!

He looked up, Lord Moore was standing before him, pale, his ordinarily firm lips trembling a little. They both of them were silent for a while; Lord Moore was trying to be calm; Garcia was looking at him with his keen dark eyes; "The lad loves her, after all, but 'tis only passion not, affection," thought he, as he looked at the pale handsome face before him. Lord Moore spoke first; his voice was very low;

"What is your reply to my suit?"

"A refusal, Lord Moore!"

"Is there no hope, then?" Demanded he; there was a sadness in his voice as he asked the question.

"You had no right, Lord Moore, to show your feelings towards my daughter to her, before speaking to me."

Lord Moore flushed up angrily, "I never spoke to her of my love," he said.

"No, you did worse, sir, you kissed her as if—" Lord Moore interrupted him hastily—"as a man his affianced wife."

"Affianced wife! Halte-là! Elle n'est pas votro fiancée encore, sauf votre respect." Garcia spoke French whenever he was excited. "Que dira votre mère? What would her ladyship say if I were to allow you to marry my daughter?"

"My mother shall welcome her, as her son's beloved wife."

"Not as a daughter of her own; she will submit to Bianca as a necessary appendage of her son. She will not love Bianca."

"What does that matter, Mr. Garcia, when I love her, and I love Bianca (his voice fell a little as he uttered the loved name) fondly, passionately, "with the love of a man!"

He spoke impetuously, but he cheek was pale. "Oh have pity on me!" He cried, his arms placed on the table and his face buried in his hand.

Garcia relented a little at this. "Let them be happy;" he thought, and sighed; "life is too short and too full of trouble. Why should I put an obstacle to their happiness." He paused;—presently;—"God help me do the right;" he said.

He glanced at the figure of Lord Moore; thou he rose and went up to him. He stood looking at him; "Good lad!" he said and touched him slightly on the arm; Lord Moore started; his pale face smote Garcia's heart.

"Poor lad!" he said again.

"Tu l'aimes bien, done."

"Plus que ma vie."

"Ta la rendras heureuse?"

"Oui, Dieu en soit temoin."

And a flush came over his pale face. "Alors, je te la donne monfils."

Garcia's eyes were misty, and he turned aside to conceal his emotion.

"Merci!" Said Lord Moore; and he wrung hard the swarthy hand of the Spanish gentleman.

"C'est assez."

There was a silence.

"Send for her, she may be crying upstairs." Said Lord Moore.

"Ay, ay, boy," then Garcia relapsed again into a deep reverie. "I wonder if I have done right" he said half to himself; "I pray God I have!"

He opened the door, and called Martha; "tell Miss Bianca to come here."

"Yes, sir."

Martha went upstairs and knocked; there was no answer she knocked again and then again; still there was silence; at length she pushed open the door and entered. Bianca was sitting by the open window.

"Why Miss Bianca,"—the girl started then shivered,—"why Miss, how pale ye are; be ye ill, deary?"

"O Martha! I feel so cold!"

"Feel cold! Why it's the hottest day we've ever had this year." Bianca rose; but she had not gone two steps, when she tottered; Martha caught her up; and led her to the sofa.

"How cold your hands are! Whatever is the mather with ye?" Said the kindly Scotch woman.

"Oh that I were dead!" Said the girl, as she sank back on the sofa. "How cold I am; am I dying Martha?"

"Dying! Whatever are yo talking about? Ye're feverish and delirious." Said Martha.

"Keep still; I shall soon be back." And quite beside herself with fright for her "deary," she hurried downstairs and into the study. "Please, sir, I believe, Miss Bianca is ill!" Said she all at once.

"Ill!" Exclaimed Garcia, "why she went out not half an hour ago from this room, and she was well then."

"But she isn't now, sir; she seems to be very ill."

Lord Moore glanced at Garcia there was reproach in his deep hazel eyes; Garcia's face grew very pale and anxious. "What is she doing now, Martha?"

"Lying on the sofa, sir, I helped her to it, she was near falling, but I held her up."

"Viens, toi," said he turning to Lord Moore; "pauvratte! j'étaus fou; j'étais trop dur." And he mounted upstairs three steps at a time, followed by Lord Moore.

V

He entered the room without stopping, making a sign to Lord Moore to stay near the door, out of sight. He went up to the touch. "Well child," said he kneeling beside her and placing his hand on her shoulder; she turned her brown eyes towards him; there was a fitful, bright, wild light in them but she recognised him;—. "C'est toi, mon père"—said she, smiling, such a strange, weird, little smile!

"Tiens!" said she, wandering a little; "j'avais commis quelque faute, n'est-ce pas? Qu'était-ce? Jo no m'en souviens pas. Qu'avais fait, mon père?"

"Rien, mon enfant, rien!"

She looked at him puzzled. Then closed her eyes and remained quiet.

"Child!"

She opened her eyes.

"Would you like to see him, my darling; would you like to see Lord Moore?"

"Ah! Chat! Hush! Do not name him; the wound is sore yet father, very sore. O God! I am *so* cold!" She went on, after a pause, her eyes dilated, and fixed toward, the window.

"It's all white with snow,—and she is so delicate; why should she lie under the earth with nothing between her and the snow but a thin plank of oak!" She half rose; "I am now like you Inez dear! Oh! that I were lying cold and still beside you under the snow!"

She lay back again; then suddenly with a piteous cry; "Don't do it again, my lord, don't. Father is so angry." She was greatly fond of poetry, and under delirium she uttered stray verses applying them to herself. "Father, it was not wrong; I love him father; he is my lion and my noble lord"—"the god of my life!"

Her eyes fell on her father, "Oh where is he? He was sitting here a minute ago, and now there's only father."

She closed her eyes again; Garcia beckoned to Lord Moore to come in; he entered and stood near the couch, silent and pale. Garcia had buried his face among the shawls; presently he raised his head and pressed the brown little hand of Bianca against his cheek.

"How hot her hand is!" He muttered.

She opened her eyes and saw Lord Moore, "How pale you are, my lord."

He dropped on his knee beside her;—"How pale you are," she said again;—"It cannot be, it cannot be!" Then she murmured in a soft clear voice,

"Ask me no more, the moon may draw the sea,
The clouds may stoop from heaven and take the shape
From fold to fold of mountain or of cape,

Yet ah! too fond when have I answered thee—

Ask me no more!

Ask me no more; thy fate and mine are sealed."

"Alas! my lord,—so it is—listen!" she said sadly.

"I strove against the stream and all in vain
Let the great river bear me to the main:

No more, dear love, for at a touch I yield

Ask me no more!"

"Inez!" She exclaimed, "did you love Ingram as much as I do my lord? yes? You were sometimes sad here, Inez. I know you were. But now you are happy dear. I should like to be with you sister."

She sighed. "Inez," she went on lower, "he kissed me Inez; was it so very wrong? Father is angry, Inez; Ingram used to kiss you sister, and father was not angry with you; I always thou he loved you best" she said sadly. "O sister; stay one minute longer, then I'll follow you."

She stopped, then went on again, "Sister! His kiss was so sweet, so strange the touch of his ups made the blood flow ruddier and stronger in my veins. 'Sweet is true love though given in vain, in vain; and sweet is death who puts an end to pain.'" She lay quiet but with her eyes open; there was a hot feverish flush on her brown cheek. She was looking steadfastly at Lord Moore: he bent down as if to kiss her;

"No, don't," thrusting him away fiercely. "It's a sin, a sin I tell you; and father is angry, and so is perhaps God;—oh! I shall never be happy again!" And she turned her face to the pillow.

Lord Moore spoke. "You must send for the doctor; shall I go?"

"Yes, yes, yes!" Said the distracted father.

VI

L ady Moore and Maggie were in the drawing room, chatting, and busy with embroidery.

"It's near eight o'clock and Henry hasn't come back yet from Mr. Garcia's, what can be the matter with him?"

"He is in love, my dear." Said Lady Moore coldly.

"Henry in love! And with whom, mamma?"

"With that Spanish girl."

"With Bianca! Oh! how nice to have Bianca for a sister!"

"I don't agree with you, Margaret; I should not like to have her as a daughter-in-law."

"Why, mamma! I thought you liked Bianca."

"One can like a girl without wishing to have her as a daughter-in-law. Bianca may be a Spanish gipsy, for aught I know."

"But you used to praise her graceful ways and manner."

"I always said she was a wild girl."

"Yes, but you said there was a natural grace in her that was quiet charming."

"I have changed my opinion now. She is not at all like what an English young lady ought to be."

"No! I suppose not! Fancy a Miss De Wilton with a pair of pistols under her outdoor jacket." And Maggie laughed at the idea. "But mamma, if Henry marries her, we can polish her up in a few days, and make her little more English!"

"Try it! She is as proud as if she were Queen of Spain. She won't submit to being polished up. She isn't pretty; I sometimes fancy she has bewitched Henry!"

"O mamma! How vexed you look! Don't you really like her then?"

"I would have liked her well enough had she left my son alone."

"I never suspected that she loved Henry." Said Maggie musingly. "No, I dare say not; she kept it close; but I saw through her artifices."

"Oh there's Henry! I must go and ask him."

"Why," she added, "he is gone straight to the stables." My lady looked out of the window. "He hasn't succeeded after all; perhaps he means to leave the country. I shall never forgive her if he does." She added, between her teeth.

Maggie had run downstairs. She found her brother busy in helping the groom to saddle the "Emperor" his favorite horse. "Henry," she said tripping up to him, "what did Bianca say?"

He turned round; she was frightened by his set, pale face.

"O Henry! What is the matter?"

"She is dying Maggie."

"Who? Bianca? Oh has there been an accident?"

Her brother was already on the saddle; he gave an impatient cut with his whip on the horse's shouldier; the spirited animal reared, his forefeet poised high up in the air; he had never received a touch of the whip; another sharp out across the shoulder, and they darted away at full gallop.

Maggie turned to the groom; "What is the matter, Sykes?"

"Dunno, miss; he came here not five minutes ago, and hordered the Hemperor to be saddled."

Maggie went upstairs to her mother. "Mamma, Bianca is very ill; oh mamma! she is dying perhaps, and we were talking lightly about her, not five minutes ago!" And the tears stood in Maggie's blue eyes. "I must go," she said, going out to bring her hat and cloak.

"No, you shall not, Margaret; stay where you are."

The girl came obediently and sat down near her mother. A servant brought a card.

"It's Mr. Owen; show him upstairs, John; Maggie, wipe your eyes and compose yourself" Maggie *had* composed herself already. She was a great favorite of Mr. Owen, and she was proud of that honour. He sat down near her, and began to talk with her mother, now and then, addressing a few words to her in a low confidential voice. He was a man of about thirty-eight or forty. Of the middle height; black hair, on which he prided himself a good deal, brushed away carefully and yet with a show of negligence from the tow brow; a nose rather snubby and fiat; thick sensual lips covered by a black moustache; and grey wicked eyes. He was esteemed very rich; and had recently come in—Shire with his family; his wife was an universal favorite; she pleased every body with her quiet gentle manners, and her sweet pretty face.

His manner was of the most pleasing kind; a little too familiar with ladies, some thought him, but generally he was liked; he so affable, so gentlemanly! my lady said,—and my lady's passport was enough to open to him all the respectable houses of the County, except that of Mr. Garcia. People wondered a little at this; but the Garcias lived so quietly; never mixed with any body since Miss Inez Garcia's death.

So after a little tittle-tattle now and anon, the subject was dropped by general consent everywhere, and Mr. Owen had free "entrée" to every house.

"He is so clever!" my lady would say, "knew everything! And seems to have travelled through all the world."

He was attentive to Margaret, and indeed to every young lady; he was fatherly with them; the very old ladies he treated with a deference, that charmed them all. He would whisper the most trival things in a manner so confidential, to a young lady, that lookers-on would think he was very intimate with her, and that they were plotting treason against some body else. Did Miss So-and-so want some monograms for her album; he moved heaven and earth to procure them, and then he would hand them to her in the most bewitching manner, and only laugh gaily at her guesses as to where he could get so many monograms; he must have a great many correspondents, and dukes, lords and knights too, as the lions rampant, the eagles soaring, the stags couchant, and the mottoes showed! He used to send for them from Rodrigues and Sons, Piccadilly, with a money order enclosed in his letter! And then he was so fond of and kind with the little girls; he was quite a favorite with children. Oh, he was a charming man!

When Lord Moore entered the sick room with Dr. Chambers, Bianca was speaking hurriedly; she did not hear the sound of the opening door, and went on incoherently.

"Pussy kiss this cross," holding out the cross which hung from her neck by a blue ribbon, "Cela te portera bonheur."

"Poor Pussy, your little Kitty has been given away; you are sorry, so am I Puss; that's right Puss, kiss the cross; He says that a sparrow does not fall to the ground without His knowledge; surely He will pity you Puss, and make you soon forgot your little one." She kissed the cross, "There I have kissed it too I and I have prayed for you, Puss; Kitty will be happy and contented in her new home."

Dr. Chambers came towards her. "Well, Miss Garcia what *are* you talking about?" Said he, with a kindly smile, fooling her pulse at the same time. "Hundred and seventy" he muttered, with his eye on his watch, "and her skin is burning hot," he added afterwards, passing his hand over the forehead where the blue veins rose and swelled as if they would burst.

"Quiet, and a soothing medicine,—Bromide of Potassium—in large doses," he said to Himself; "how long has she been ill?" aloud and distinctly, turning to Garcia.

"Not four hours yet."

"She must have been greatly excited to be thus delirious. What excited her!"

Garcia did not reply.

"Ah well!" Said Dr. Chambers after a silence, "you must keep her very quiet, and give her this every hour till she becomes calm."

He prescribed and thou went away; Lord Moore went out too, and too minutes after came back with the medicine. Her father made her drink one dose. She lay pretty quiet after that, sometimes only she uttered one or two incoherent sentences. One hour passed and another dose was given. That had more effect, she became drowsy. Lord Moore rose. It was past ten P.M.

"I must go now!" he said in a low voice; he went softly to the couch, stooped down and kissed the flushed, feverish cheek.

"Another Will," she murmured sleepily, and then added very low indeed "for Montague's sake." He kissed her again, and silently wringing the hand of Mr. Garcia galloped home. He went to his study; his mother was waiting there for him. He came and leant against the mantly-shelf, his face pale and gloomy.

"Well" said Lady Moore, after a long silence, seeing he did not speak.

"She is dying mother." He said bitterly.

"Perhaps that is the best thing she could do, put herself out of my son's way!" She spoke harshly; Lord Moore's despair even goaded her to speak thus. She hated the girl for being the cause of her son's estrangement from her, his own mother. Why should that girl stand between her son and his family, his ambition, his happiness?

Lord Moore buried his face in his hands, without replying. "God have mercy upon me and spare her." He cried, from the bottom of his heart. Lady Moore stayed some minutes more, then went out, softly. His grief frightened her into awe, if not into sympathy.

VII

Days and weeks the girl lay tossing in her bed of illness. She took very little nourishment; a doctor from London was sent for; there were moments when all hope for her life was given up. Garcia wrote to her maternal aunt Dorothy, now Mrs. Cranly, a widow. She was very fond of Bianca, and not only loved but esteemed her highly; she came at once to nurse her. Bianca would, in her delirium, call back things that happened long ago, when she was a girl.

Once, she started up with fierce angry eyes; "Laissez-la aller, je vous le répète, ou je vous tue!"

And she put up her hands as though in the act of levelling a pistol at somebody; she dropped her hands presently, with a smile of cool sarcasm, "c'est un poltron, après tout."

Then she would go back to her still earlier days; "Inez je te demande pardon; j'avais tort do m'emportor comme ça, je crois ce que tu dis!"

She would say, penitently, "N'en parlons plus ma sœur." Then she would say—"Pauvre sœur! elle est morte si jeune, si jeune; pourquoi est-ello morte, elle, si bonne, si belle,—couronnéo do l'astre do la nuit." Then sighing,

> "Elle avait tant d'espoir ea entrant dons le monde
> Orguoilleuse et los yeux baissés."
> "C'estmoi qui aurait dû mourir."

The father keeping watch night and day, would sometimes get angry with Lord More, and reproach him as being the root.

"He is the cause," Garcia would think sitting gloomily by the bed. "Would to God he had never crossed my threshold! She would have lived contented and happy with her old father, without giving one thought to other love. She would have lived quietly and in calm happiness all the days of her life with me, with never a thought for anybody else; and now, my sole darling, my last and best, is dying for aught I know; she is leaving me as the others have done. I shall be very lonely then. I shall die like a rat in a hole without one dear being to close my fading eyes."

And Garcia would walk away, and his heart would sink at the thought of all this.

Lord Moore came often daily; He would enquire below; he was not allowed to go upstairs now; Mrs. Cranly took a great fancy to him. She, with her woman's keen eyes, saw how matters stood before Garcia breathed a word; and she was delighted to have a lord for a relative, even by marriage, only she thought that Bianca was too good for him; an emperor even, would hardly in her opinion, have been worthy of Bianca. She would talk to Lord Moore by the hour, speaking about Bianca and her pretty ways when a child of between four and six.

Once, when the London doctor even, gave up all hope, Garcia called in Lord Moore. "Viens la voir pour la dernière fois" said he hoarsely.

They both entered the dim and darkened room. The dawn was just breaking; the coming sun, shed a ruddy blush over the elm-tree tops. The bed had been wheeled towards the window. She was lying with her face towards the window, her large brown eyes fixed on the fields beyond. Mrs. Cranly was sitting quietly by the pillow, silently wiping away the tears that flowed down both her own cheeks. Garcia and Lord Moore went by the bed and stood near; Garcia knelt down at the foot, his hands pressed together in agonised prayer.

"Look, father, the sun is rising so beautifully this morning." Said Bianca. "Do you remember Theuriet's description of dawn?" and she murmured softly:

> "Je m'endors, et là-bas lo frissonnant matin
> Baigne les ampers verts d'une rougeur furtive,
> Et toujours cette odeur amoureuse m'arrive
> Avec le dernier chant d'un rossignol lointain
> Et les premiers cris de la grive. . ."

"It's a sad story, father, isn't it?" She closed her eyes and fell into a sort of drowsy stupor.

It was on an evening in the latter part of July that Bianca first began to recover. Garcia had been sitting by the bed wrapt in a sad and depressing reverie; buried in his own thoughts he murmured to himself unconsciously,

> "Departed the crown of his glory
> No wife and no children to clasp!"

A sob startled him; he turned towards the bed, "Bianca!"

She turned round, after a moment's delay; she had wiped away the recent tears, but the traces remained. He took her hand in his.

"Father;" she said, and her voice trembled; "don't say that; I shall never leave you; I shall always be with you."

Her brown eyes were shining lucid and calm through her rising tears.

"Will you Bianca?"

"Yes, father."

There was a silence.

Garcia was humbly thanking God for his mercy.

"But father, why are you sitting here?"

"You have been very ill, Bianca."

"Have I? And you have been keeping awake at night. Now that's very wrong, father; you must go to bed."

"It's only nine o'clock now, child."

"Never mind; how long have I been ill?"

"More than a month now, Bianca."

"And you have been fretting about me, all this time!" She exclaimed. "That's too bad. Now go to bed, this instant, like a good boy, father! Indeed I shall never sleep if you keep awake." And she tried to sit up. "How weak I am!" She said, and lay down again. "Father; now do go to bed. If you fall ill, who will take care of me?" He was obliged to go away to his own room.

The next morning, very early, when Martha came to Bianca's room, her joy knew no bounds when she saw her young mistress "like her dear own sel' agin." When Garcia entered his daughter's room, he found her, dressed in a neat print dressing-gown; her black hair was brushed away smoothly (she was too weak to be able to bind it) behind her small ears. She looked very pale and thin, but a quiet happy smile came on her lips when her father entered.

"Why! Up and dressed already, Bianca!" He exclaimed.

"I was too weak to dress, father, so I put on this dressing-gown."

"There is somebody waiting outside to see you."

"The doctor?"

"Mieux que ça. Somebody who loves you a good deal and whom you love too."

"Ah! I have heard it all from Martha, father. It's aunt Dorothy."

"Mieux que ça." Said he laughing; "the person is much taller than Aunt Dorothy, and somewhat dearer, I take it; his name begins with an M." A faint flush came into the pale cheeks.

"You have guessed at last, I see" said Garcia, laughing. "Come in, Henry."

She turned her eyes towards the door. Lord Moore came in, took her hand in his, and stooping down kissed her on the forehead. She glanced up hastily at her father, with a frightened look in her eyes.

"Ay, ay; let the lad kiss you, child; there's no harm in it now. Give her another kiss, lad, to reassure her."

And he laughed but his eyes were wet. She shrank away so timidly at her father's words, that Lord Moore, only smiled gravely to encourage her. He had her hand in his and he looked at the white thin fingers sadly, as they lay against his own strong ones.

"You must be quick and get well, Bianca," said her father, "look Henry is regarding with sorrow your thin little hands; you must pick up flesh, and get strong again."

"Yes, father." Then after a pause.

"Do you like my lord, now father?" She asked anxiously,

"Not a bit, Bianca;" said Garcia, as he placed his hand on Lord Moore's shoulder; who smiled. "But I suppose I must bring myself to like him, since you love him so much, child."

She glanced at him and seeing he was jesting, made him sit beside her and took his hand in hers.

"Father; you are very good." And the tears came into her eyes.

"Now don't cry or you'll be ill again; I shall go and bring you your breakfast. Henry shall keep you company, till I return; and mind no tears or excitement," and with that he went out.

She followed him fondly with her eyes, till he shut the door after him, then she looked at Lord Moore. "Father is very good, my lord." She said simply.

"Yes, Bianca." His gentle tones, for he had not spoken since he entered, his calling her by her Christian name, made her start and flush up. He saw it, and bending down; "Your father has consented Bianca to give you to me; do you consent also to be my wife?" said he softly.

She bent her head meekly. She took his hand and pressed her lips on it. That was her only reply. She was too happy to speak.

He kissed the bended head solemnly and tenderly. "My beloved wife!"

"My noble lord!"

This was how they plighted their troth. They did not speak much at first; His hand clasped hers in a strung tender clasp. Presently he broke the silence. "Bianca" (how sweet her name sounded pronounced by his lips) "you must get well very fast: I am anxious to take my bride home to my father's house." He added, smiling. Her heart sank a little. "And my father, my lord," said she with an unsteady voice. "He will live with us Bianca."

She shook her head sadly. "He will never live with Lady Moore."

"But it's not to the old house we are going; my mother and Maggie will live there; we are going to Montague House in Wales; your father will stay there with us; I have arranged it all with him; I knew he could not live without his Bianca." And he smiled.

"How kind you are, my lord!"

"You mustn't call me, my lord, any more, Bianca," smiling and passing his hand over her hair.

"What shall I call you, my lord?"

"There! you've said it again! But you pronounce it so prettily, that I have hardly the heart to forbid you. But my mother would curl her lip if she heard you call me so, now that we are betrothed; she would say you wore 'a romantic young chit.'"

"But you are *my* lord now more than ever." She replied with a proud, happy smile "Henry? Every body calls you Henry!"

"Well then the other name,"—smiling; "you like Montague I know."

"How do you know that, my lord?"

"Why; once while you were delirious you asked Will to kiss you for Montague's sake."

"Did I?" and a faint flush came to her cheeks. "Did Will come to see me?"

"No; it wasn't Will; it was Will's brother," smiling "who kissed you before he went away, and you asked for another, 'for Montague's sake'!"

The dark blood had suffused her cheeks and forehead; her eyes were bright and happy. "In truth fair Montague, I am too fond." Said she laughing, but the tears came to her eyes; "I am so happy, that they will come" said she half-ashamed and wiping them away hastily. "For Montague's sake then, my lord," said she with a childish gesture, smiling; he kissed her on the mouth, nothing loth.

When her father came in, she turned to him with a frank yet bashful smile; "Lord Moore has told me all, my father." And she pressed Garcia's hand in her own, She bade her take her breakfast, and was only half-pleased as she only drank a single cup of tea, and sent away the tray.

"What!" he cried, "is that what you call, a breakfast!"

"Indeed, father, I cannot eat any more today; you know that when one is excited, solid food seems to stick in one's throat."

"Nonsense! Then you must not be excited. Rest and proper nourishment are the only things to set you up again!"

"At luncheon, father I am not hungry now, and cannot take any thing more at present."

VIII

"I cannot think what can be the matter with Henry, he seems quite changed and happy of late." The speaker was Lady Moore, the listener was Mr. Owen.

My lady had a strong regard for his good sense and latterly that feeling had been increased by Mr. Owen's regularly attending my lady's weekly prayer-meeting; for my lady was a "dévote."

"Depend on it madam, he is in love"—was the laconic answer, then looking around, "I hope innocent little Miss Margaret is not hidden somewhere."

"No. She is too far off to be able to hear Mr. Owen. She is gone to see her dear friend, Miss Garcia."

There was a pause.

"So Miss Margaret has followed her brother's example and fallen in love with the gipsy queen!" He laughed a forced hard laugh. My lady wondered at the acuteness of Mr. Owen.

"You seem to know everything, Mr. Owen."

"I always keep my eyes open, Lady Moore; and if I may speak out; I see this love-affair in a very suspicious light."

"How lightly you speak! Henry is too much set on it, he will end by marrying that girl," and my lady sighed. "Is your ladyship averse to the match?" The question was asked in an eager, anxious manner though Mr. Owen tried hard to appear calm as usual.

"Yes. I shall do anything to help your ladyship, for I do not think it on any account a desirable marriage."

"Will you try and help me?"

"With all my heart. I am under deep obligations to your ladyship. Can I ever forget who first lighted up for me the mysteries of this book"—and he solemnly touched a Bible, lying on Lady Moore's work—table.

My lady smiled grimly, greatly flattered. Poor Lady Moore! Not even you, with all your acuteness, were able to penetrate into the heart of Mr. Owen;—if he had one, winch is, dour reader, very much to be doubted.

The ladies had just left the table, and Lord Moore was sitting alone with Mr. Owen. The former was peeling a peach carefully and slowly, as though his thoughts were elsewhere. Mr. Owen was sipping champagne and keeping a steady eye on Lord Moore's face. Lord Moore left the peach untasted on his plate, and rising went to the window.

"It is a fine night, I think I'll take a walk." Said he. Mr. Owen came behind him and put his hand in a kind elder—brotherly way on my lords shoulder.

"I know where you are going cousin!" Said he laughing, then taking a serious air; "You'd better take care!"

"What do you mean?" Said Lord Moore, moving further off a little; Owen's familiar manner irritated him. Mr. Owen shifted his ground, and spoke half—jestingly.

"I have seen you lately enter a certain house, and I wondered what could make you so assiduous in your visits. I have found the clue."

"You watched me!"

"No indeed, how can you say that?" In a tone of mild reproach.

"Who told you then, Mr. Owen?"

"My wife; She saw a pretty brown-eyed dark-haired damsel in the garden of that certain house, and of course, as a dutiful wife, told me about it."

"Do you know the Garcias?"

Mr. Owen smiled; it was a shrewd smile; it seemed to imply, "I should not like to have that honour." he hoped Lord Moore would see that smile, but he was disappointed. Then he only said, "No. I should like to know them very much. But is that Miss Garcia, with the dark-brown eyes and the low forehead?"

"Yes."

"What is her name? Has she no sister or brother?"

"No. Bianca is her name."

Mr. Owen gave a little start, and looked up at Lord Moore, but he had his eyes fixed beyond, on the yellow fields of corn which looked beautiful under the moon's pale beams, like a rippling sea of gold.

"And a very pretty name it is." Then he sighed. "I am afraid your mother will hardly approve of your choice though, when she hears of it."

"She knows about it already."

"And has given her consent?" with an air of surprised pleasure.

"Not yet; and she may be so long in giving it, that I think I shall do without it. I can't wait."

"Ah! youth! youth! youth! ever impetuous, never patient." And Mr. Owen sighed again.

"Shall we go upstairs Mr. Owen?"

"With all my heart."

They went into the drawing-room. Maggie was at the piano trilling a merry ditty in her sweet voice. My lady was near the window; she was embroidering. Another lady was sitting beside her on the ottoman. This lady was younger, about thirty years old; her brown, thin, silky hair was brushed away from the broad white forehead, her small mouth with its mobile lips denoted a soft, yielding nature; her dark grey eyes, large, sweet, patient had something sad in them. This was Mrs. Owen. Mr. Owen went to the piano and stood behind Maggie's stool, turning the leaves for her. Lord Moore went and sat beside Mrs. Owen.

"I hope little Helen and the baby are quite well, Mrs. Owen?" He asked in his kind manly voice.

Mrs. Owen looked up at him gratefully, "Yes, thank you; Helen is very fond of your brother; she is always asking about little Willie."

There was a pause.

"I suppose Willie is gone to bed?" Asked Mrs. Owen. "Yes, he must be fast asleep long ere now." A second pause. Lord Moore broke the silence.

"Do you know the Garcias Mrs. Owen?" He asked carelessly.

"Yes—no—yes—at least I used to know them. But we never meet them now." Stammered Mrs. Owen. She had a nervous way of clasping and unclasping her fingers when excited.

Lord Moore saw that the subject somehow distressed her and talked about other things, children principally, for Mrs. Owen was a very fond mother. From time to time Mrs. Owen cast a furtive glance towards the group near the piano, and bye and bye, her replies and remarks to Lord Moore were given in an absent manner. She was thinking of other things. Maggie was turning over the leaves of a music book, Mr. Owen was bending over her and whispering to her things which made her laugh, and strike him playfully on the arm with her small white hand.

"Now, Mr. Owen, you will make me die of laughing."

"Mr. Owen! Why will you never call me Cousin or Mark; we are such near relations, sweet coz now sing me this;" pointing to the well—known song of Ben Jonson "Drink to me only with thine eyes."

She began the song, but after the first line stopped; "Now *Cousin*, you must not look at me so, you put me out." He smiled, patted her on the shoulder in a fatherly way, and sat down on a chair. Mrs. Owen rose. "It's near nine o'clock, Mark, shall we go?"

"If you like, love, ah Mary, I know why you wish to go so soon, it's all for the sake of little Helen."

Mrs. Owen smiled, a quiet, sad smile it was. They bade good-night to the ladies. Lord Moore accompanied them part of the way. On his way home, he passed the small house of Garcia, and lingered a moment, smoking his cigar thoughtfully.

"Now quiet all around is!" Said he. "How peaceful, how refreshing the night is!"

A month after, two horses were waiting at the door of Mr. Garcia's house. Beautiful animals they were. A dark hay and a chestnut. The chestnut was saddled for a lady. Presently Bianca came down the steps, followed by Lord Moore. She came and patted both the horses. Garcia was looking on from his study window.

"Take care, Bianca, the chestnut seems a little too fiery."

"So much the better, father."

"She is gentle as a lamb, Bianca, or I would not have trusted you to her." Said Lord Moore, as he stooped down to help her into her saddle.

She looked very pretty, on the whole, in her dark blue habit, and her Spanish hat surmounted by a black ostrich feather. Lord Moore sprung on his saddle, and they went off. The first mile they kept close to each other, side by side, galloping at full speed across open meadows, he smiling and sometimes clasping her hand. She looked a little too slim and pale; she had not yet quite recovered her strength; but the exercise and the fresh air soon brought the blood to her cheeks.

After a ride of two hours they came back to Moorehouse. She placed her small brown hand very lightly on his shoulder as he helped her down. She was just patting the horse when she heard a sudden joyous cry of "Bianca." She turned round, but Willie had hidden himself behind his brother who catching him in his arms, placed him on the saddle. Willie was delighted.

"Walk the ho'ss." He said in his royal way.

"You hold Will, my lord, and I'll take the bridle;" said Bianca. They were all three laughing gaily when three equestrians entered the yard. it was Mr. and Mrs. Owen and Margaret. Bianca stopped; all her merriment died out of her face. Mr. Owen had lighted on the ground and was helping the ladies to dismount.

He turned towards Bianca, and bowed with a polite smile on his lips, "I have the pleasure to speak with Miss Garcia, I believe." Bianca turned her eyes towards him, a scornful smile parted her lips.

"We broke off all connection with you Mr. Owen, long ago, I do not wish to renew it," and she walked away. She had barely reached the end of the avenue, when Lord Moore joined her.

"Why are you so angry? Don't you know he is my cousin?"

"Je ne vous on fais pas mon compliment," in a cool sarcastic voice.

"Bianca!" his tender, yet reproachful tone at her cold manner, smote her to the quick.

Impetuously she put both her hands into his; "I was wrong to speak to you so; will my lord pardon me?"

"Pardon you what, my Bianca?" smiling and stooping down to kiss her forehead.

She clasped his hand closer, and spoke earnestly; "My lord, take care of that man; he is a bold bad man. He mustn't come here often."

He smiled at her tone of command. "What do you know against him, Bianca? Many things, eh?"

"One thing, my lord," she replied, "but that is enough."

"You puzzle me, Bianca, with your severe haughty little face."

She shook her head, as if hurt at his somewhat light tone. "Goodbye" she said.

"What, going already?"

"Yes, I hate that man, and father and I do not wish to know him, or any of his family any more." Then after a pause. "Mrs. Owen is a distant relative of ours. I wonder she has married him, after all his wicked doings; but she was always gentle, and loved him, bad as he is, with all her faithful, womanly heart." She spoke hurriedly and with a heightened color; Lord Moore understood her.

"But perhaps he has turned a new leaf, Bianca; he attends church regularly, and seems very religiously inclined."

She smiled, a fine little smile which said a great deal. He accompanied her part of the way; but she sent him back.

IX

He was going away. The Crimean war had broken out and England required her sons to do their duty. Lord Moore was a captain in the regiment and he was leaving England for Sevastopol.

It was their last day. He was sitting beside her in the garden covered with dead leaves. She held his hand in her small brown one, firmly, tenderly; her eyes fixed on Lord Moore's face. Every lineament of that dear face was being engraved in her heart. He must go, but the parting was hard, very hard. Presently he took off a small ring from his watch-guard, and slid it on her marriage finger. "You will wear that for my sake, darling, and if I never return—"

Her downcast eyelids quivered.*

---

* The gentle hand that had traced the story thus far—the hand of Miss Toru Dutt—left off here. Was it illness that made the pen drop from the weary fingers? I do not know. I think not. The sketch was a draft attempt probably, and abandoned. I am inclined to think so because the novel left in the French language; very much superior indeed to this fragment and is complete. Other fragments there are both in prose and verse but mostly rough hewn and unpolished.

A Note About the Author

Toru Dutt (1856–1877) was a Bengali poet and translator. Born in Calcutta to a prominent family of Bengali Christians, Dutt was educated from a young age and became a devoted student of English literature. Taught by her father and a private tutor, she learned French, Sanskrit, and English in addition to her native Bengali. At thirteen, she left India with her family to travel through Europe, visiting France, England, Italy, and Germany over the next several years. In 1872, she attended a series of lectures for women at the University of Cambridge alongside her sister Aru, which further sparked her interest in academia and literature. In 1873, the family returned to Calcutta, where Dutt struggled to readjust to Indian culture. She wrote two novels in English and French before publishing *A Sheaf Gleaned in French Fields* (1876), a collection of French poems translated into English. Its critical and commercial success came tragically late, however, as Dutt died of consumption in 1877 at the age of 21. She has since been recognized as the first Indian writer to publish a novel in French, the first Indian woman to publish an English novel, and a pioneering figure in Anglo-Indian literature whose mastery of several languages at such a young age remains remarkably uncommon. *Ancient Ballads and Legends of Hindustan* (1882), a collection of Sanskrit poems translated into English, was her final, posthumously published work.

A Note from the Publisher

Spanning many genres, from non-fiction essays to literature classics to children's books and lyric poetry, Mint Edition books showcase the master works of our time in a modern new package. The text is freshly typeset, is clean and easy to read, and features a new note about the author in each volume. Many books also include exclusive new introductory material. Every book boasts a striking new cover, which makes it as appropriate for collecting as it is for gift giving. Mint Edition books are only printed when a reader orders them, so natural resources are not wasted. We're proud that our books are never manufactured in excess and exist only in the exact quantity they need to be read and enjoyed.

bookfinity™

Discover more of your favorite classics with Bookfinity™.

- Track your reading with custom book lists.
- Get great book recommendations for your personalized Reader Type.
- Add reviews for your favorite books.
- AND MUCH MORE!

Visit **bookfinity.com** and take the fun Reader Type quiz to get started.

Enjoy our classic and modern companion pairings!

Classic & Modern

Printed in the USA
CPSIA information can be obtained
at www.ICGtesting.com
JSHW080007150824
68134JS00021B/2335

9 781513 299983